Stewart and the Forest Creature

CRAZY HORSE PRESS

www.crazyhorsepress.com

By Peter Hayden:
The Adventures of Stringy Simon series, vol. 1 - 6
The Headmaster's Daughter
The Day Trip
And Smith Must Score...
Sorting the Apples & Pears
The Poppy Factory Takeover

J210,861
£7.70

CRAZY HORSE PRESS

53 Stourport Road
BEWDLEY
DY12 1BH

[+44 (0)1299 403201]
phayden@crazyhorsepress.com
www.crazyhorsepress.com

Text © Peter Hayden 2005
Illustration © Clinton Banbury 2005

ISBN 1 871870 24 0

Printed by T. Snape & Co Ltd. Boltons Court, Preston PR1 3TY [01772 254553]

About this book...

"Hello there...

Stringy Simon, Patsy and Stewart have just got back from staying with their friends the Murdochs in Australia.

Stewart is an unusual kid because he gets to choose his birthdays. In Volume 1 he chose April 1st – which he calls *Fish Finger Day* because of something he read in the library. But Stewart is a cunning kid, and he has figured out how to con an extra birthday out of his parents.

As you read the stories you will realise Stewart has quite a lot of birthdays. In fact, by the end of Volume 6 he is ready for secondary school, and he's become a bit of a street-smart kid. So please note – Volume 6 contains some rude words.

If this is your friend's book and you want your own, just cut out the order form from the back and send it – or get someone to photocopy it for you to send. You can have your book signed if you want, it tells you how on the form.

Enjoy the stories."

Peter Hayden.

Did you know you can get Stringy Simon books for £3.50 if you're clever... Go to the Discount Order Form at the back...

Contents

For Ben and Mike

Chapter 29
FROGGY'S LITTLE MISTAKE

Before you start this story, read page iii at the front.

Sun sets in the west. So when it came time for true blue dinky-di Stewart and our Pommie friends to leave their mates the Murdochs, they flew into the most beaut Aussie sunset you've ever seen.

Sunset is nature's signal that night's on the way, it's time to get some kip. But this sunset was different - it wouldn't go down. The plane was moving so fast it chased it right round the world, over Asia, India, Arabia, Europe, till it finally plonked them back in England and darkness settled in. The holiday was over.

Wearily they heaved their bags and caught the late train. They were so tired they were past sleep - felt like they were awake the *other* side of sleep instead of this side. When they stared out the windows looking for things, they just saw their own eyes gaping back like gongs.

The taxi-man drove as fast as he could. He didn't fancy trying to wake them if they dozed off in his cab, but by their street there was a barrier and he had to stop.

A policeman tapped the window.

'Sorry sir, bit of a hold-up. Road-works. Have to go round I'm afraid.'

Finally, after a last-minute detour, they made it home to bed.

*   *   *   *   *

Now, since our globe-trotting chums are catching a bit of shut-eye, it gives me the chance to tell you a rather *interesting fact* about Stewart.

He had four birthdays in a year.

Wanna bet?

Give your teacher a pound before you read the next bit. Or your parent, if you're at home. That's your bet. If I prove it, I've won. They've got to send me the pound. If I don't, you've won, and they give you the pound back plus another one, and I'll pay them next time I see them. Deal?

Deal.

You see, Stewart was a nativity baby - born on Christmas Eve. As we know, mid-December is a bad time to be born, cause you might get a combined birthday-and-Christmas present instead of two separate ones. That's O.K., cause it's usually bigger. But after you're about five they seem to forget – or maybe think you've forgotten. You end up with one small pressie and that's yer lot.

Stringy Simon and Patsy knew about this. Their idea was to let Stewart choose a birthday himself. So he would have Christmas presents at Christmas-time and birthday presents on his chosen birthday. And Stewart figured he could do better if he changed it each year, to keep them on their toes.

If an uncle happened to get a *tax rebate*, or win the competition in the paper, that would be a good time to announce your birthday. Whereas if their tele packed up or their *M.O.T.* was due, that would be a dumb time.

Stewart was no fool. He'd had one birthday – April first, the fish-finger one*. The year went round to winter and they went to Aussie-land, where it was summer. When they were back he picked his time.

'Um – in Australia it was summer, right? But here it's winter... So - was it last summer or next summer?'

That got them. A little argument started. Stewart waited, then asked an easier question. Like Mrs Hodgetts did in class.

'When you phone them from England – is it the day before or the day after?'

* [See 'Stewart Picks a Birthday' – Volume 1]

Took a long time, cause they weren't the brightest class. This is the answer: if you phone on Saturday, it's Sunday in Australia – so it must be the day after.

'That means it was *next* summer,' he said when the penny dropped, 'so I've decided my birthday was the day we landed in Sydney. You all forgot, now you owe me a present.'

'But... your real one was only a couple of days after... That's two in a week.' Patsy was flummoxed.

'Can have them close if I want...' said Stewart.

'But... How can your *next* birthday be before your last birthday?'

'Australia,' he said quick. 'Upside-down land. Tell you what - I'll accept one present from all of you. 'Kay?'

That's how he managed to land himself a spanking new mountain bike - joint present from Stringy Simon, Portly Paul, Patsy and Bertha.

Don't forget the pound...

Three hundred and sixty-five days a year, right? That takes you from Christmas *Day* to the next Christmas *Eve* – and Stewart had three birthdays. First of April, fish-finger one; landing day in Sydney, next year's one; and his real one, Christmas Eve.

But... some years have three hundred and sixty-*six* days, that means you can count from the Christmas Eve before. Stewart's birthday.

Four birthdays, three hundred sixty-six days. One year.

Pound coins only please, don't send change.

*   *   *   *   *

He thought of keeping his bike in the garage, but the door was wonky. Someone could break in with a couple of shoves. So he lugged it to his bedroom, and used his new combination *anti-thief* lock to clamp it to the radiator pipe.

'My bike', he said chirpily, soon as he woke the next day. 'I'll unlock it and have a ride round.'

He flung on some clothes and started to do the lock.

'Now let's see,' he said. 'Two-one-six-six.' It was a bit stiff. 'No, six-six-one-two.... one-six...'

Soon he was in a right muddle. There were sixes and ones and twos coming out his ears, but it still wouldn't open. He was stuck - and the only one who could unstick him was Sid the Plumber.

'Well, well well,' said Sid, when he came round. 'Looks like you've *saddled* yourself with a bit of a problem, m'n!' He was one for the gags, was Sid. Welsh. 'Are you sure you haven't got the numbers upside-down after all that time in Aussie-land? Try two-one-nine-nine. If not it'll have to be the cutters.'

From Llangadwaladr, I believe. Or was it Llanfaelog..?

Stewart tried everything - nines, sixes, twos - he was that confused he tried Barry Penwallet's phone number. But none of them worked, and Sid had to get the cutters after all. They were massive, looked like they could cut through the trans-Atlantic telephone cable, never mind Stewart's bike-lock. But no matter how Sid tried he couldn't get it apart. It was an anti-thief device alright - needed a stick of dynamite to bust it.

Sid scratched his head.

'It's no good,' he said, 'I'll have to cut the pipe instead.'

Well, you can't just cut a radiator-pipe, you'd get hot water everywhere. First you've got to *drain the system*, and that's what Sid did.

He loosened the radiator and fixed a hose to the pipe. He hung the other end out the window and sent the lot gushing into the garden - the heating water from the entire house. Soon there was nothing but steam. Felt like they were in one of those places where hot water bubbles out of the earth.

When it was done, Sid got Stewart to help him lug the radiator down while he dealt with the pipe. But Stewart realised you could just slip the anti-thief lock over it now without cutting at all.

'Ah,' said Sid thoughtfully, 'that's not what I meant, see. I meant I'd have to cut through your *bicycle frame* pipe, otherwise you'll be trailing that thing round wherever you go.'

Stewart looked at his bike-frame. Sure enough the only way was to cut through, slide the lock off, and weld it back again.

'Two-one-six-nine!' he yelled, as Sid was thumbing the blade of his fret-saw. He'd remembered! Fancy that. Like a chap in a torture chamber remembers when he catches sight of the implements.

With a click it was off.

'Better help me put this lot back again, hadn't you,' said Sid raising an eyebrow. And they went to fetch the radiator.

*   *   *   *   *

Good job they did, too, cause after that there was a cold snap for a while. Didn't snow but it was well cold. There were thick white frosts, and the heating stayed on all the time.

It worked O.K., but not as well as before. You could hear it gurgling. It never stopped. Rble, rble, rble, specially in Stewart's room. They got Sid to take another look.

He had a cup of tea and scratched his head.

'No good,' he said, 'I'll have to drain the system again.'

He undid the radiator and hosed the water out like before. Then set about tapping the pipes. Tap, tap, clank. Tap, tap, clank. He worked his way along the system. Down the landing, into the bathroom. Stewart stayed on his bunk, waiting for him to tap his way back.

'Oi,' came a little voice, 'what's the noise about?'

Stewart leaned over, and there, in the cup-shape where the radiator-pipe widened to join the main pipe, were two shiny eyes.

'Froggy!' whispered Stewart. 'What are you doing? You've bunged the system up.'

'Hmph. I like that,' he said grumpily. 'Chap goes to take a warm bath, next thing you know he's lugged upstairs and shut in the pipes half the week. I'm cooked.'

Stewart sat up excitedly, dangling his legs. 'You can talk!'

'Course I can talk. You'd learn to talk if you were stuck in a pipe all day, nothing to do but listen. Couldn't even turn round. I was just thinking about a nice hibernation when the tapping started up. What was it anyway?'

Tap, tap, tap, clank. He was coming back along.

'Quick, the plumber,' said Stewart. 'Hide if you don't want to be flushed down the loo.'

Tap, tap, clank. Tap, tap, clank. Tap, tap, tap, tap. Tap, tap, tap. Tap.

'Hmn. Seems to have cleared itself.' said Sid, coming in. 'Must have had a bit of an *air-block*. Well, best fasten things up and be on my way.'

* * * * *

'Wow!' said Stewart when he'd gone. 'Fancy *evesdropping* for nearly a week. Pity you weren't in the staffroom one at school, you might have heard where they keep our marleys when they take them off us. What d'you hear then, anything interesting?'

'Yes,' said Froggy, 'I heard you've been on holiday and you came back on the win wan wine.'

'Wine?' said Stewart 'Oh. *Railway line.* Yes, we came home on the railway line, then a taxi.'

'Heard you fall out your bunk the other day and bang your forest,' said Froggy.

'Forest?' said Stewart. 'Oh. *Forehead.* Yes, I thought I was still in Australia. Forgot about the bunk and banged my forehead.'

'And I hear you're having cobs on the webs for supper. Sounds good to me, I haven't had a feed for a week.'

'Cobs on the webs?' said Stewart. 'Cobs on the webs? Oh. *Corn on the cob.* Yes, we're having corn on the cob, with butter. No spiders though. Sorry.'

Froggy was good alright, but not that good. He seemed to get the odd word wrong each time. He looked at Stewart in his froggy way, and knew what he was thinking. I'll show him, he thought, he won't think I get words wrong when I say the next thing I heard.

'Rebet,' he said. 'You think they're mending the road, don't you?' He was on the window-ledge now, looking out. 'Well they're not. They're building a duck-hole, that's what they're doing. I heard 'em.'

Stewart was astonished.

'Duck-hole?' he said. 'You mean a pond? They can't build one here, how will people get to the shop. We won't be able to sell our toys...'

'Don't know about that,' Froggy said, 'but they're building a duck-hole, I heard a man say before you shut me in the pipes. "Sorry about the duck-hole," he said, "you'll have to go round".'

'But you couldn't talk then,' said Stewart.

'Ah, but I can now, and that's what he said.' Froggie was *adamant*.

The grown ups were furious. They wrote letters to the Mayor and kicked up a stink. They got the papers round. *DUCK-HOLE IS A QUACKPOT IDEA*, said the headline. *TOY HOSPITAL MAY CLOSE.*

There was an outcry. People came with placards. They booed the diggers and banged on their toilet booth while they were inside.

The mayor put his chain on and went to inspect the roadworks himself. 'There are no plans for a duck pond,' he roared at the newsmen. 'I categorically deny it.'

They charged to the shop, kicking bollards and safety lamps, and rapped the door. Stewart opened it. 'Who is your informant?' they yelled. 'Who's the *mole* in the Town Hall?'

Stewart was amazed. They find out everything.

'Um, not a mole,' he said. 'Frog actually. He heard one of them say....'

'WOW!' Their pens went berserk. They got every word he said. And printed it.

TOY-SHOP LOONIES TALK TO FROGS, the front pages said. *TOAD-IN-THE-PIPE BOY TELLS ALL.*

*   *   *   *   *

Things weren't too *comfortable* for Stewart after that. Instead of riding his bike proudly round town, he was sent to his room in disgrace.

'You got me in big trouble Froggy,' he whispered when it was safe to talk. 'Tell me what you heard again, really slowly...'

Froggie blinked and thought a minute.

'"Sorry sir, bit of a duck-hole. Have to go round."' Froggie was scared of ducks himself, horrid things with beaks. He understood the policeman exactly.

'Duck-hole. Duck-hole...' thought Stewart. And suddenly it was clear. 'Hold-up.... that's what you heard. Sorry about the *hold-up*. You got it back to front, you daft penny-worth.'

He looked a long time at froggie's face.

'I'd quit the area if I were you,' he said after a bit. 'They'll chop you up and feed you to the birds if they catch you.'

Froggie did a swallow.

'This *Hop*-stralia place you went to,' he said. 'Is it very far...?'

Chapter 30
DOUGLAS THE DOGLESS

Stewart was in Cubs. His Akela was Jewel. Jewel had red lips and a loud voice, and bossed them all the time. Stewart loved her nearly as much as Mrs Hodgetts.

All the cubs' parents loved her too. Most akelas do brilliant games like indoor hockey and off-ground-he, but send you home with bruises and dirty uniforms. Your parents moan all night. Or stop you going. But Jewel was different. She was a badge-merchant. She was well into badges. You could say she was badge-mad.

You might think this would be a bit of a boring pack, sitting round tying knots and stuff for badges. The heck it was. They had the best games of bulldog for miles. They charged and smashed each other all night. Knees got twisted, shoes went flying, and over it all Jewel'ud be shrieking, 'Get him down! Grab his ear!' When the games ended the kids would collapse in exhaustion. There'd be ripped pockets, knees weeping and bleeding, uniforms covered with cack off the floor.

This was where Jewel came up trumps. While the kids were counting their teeth, she'd get started. Out came the tables. Sewing table, with needles and thread, spare

buttons, zips, trouser patches. Ironing table with state-of-the-art steam iron. It was that powerful it could flatten the creases in a corrugated fence, never mind a cub shirt. There was a Fairy Liquid table, for sponging dirt and blood, first-aid table, brush and comb table with a big mirror, shoe-polish table and a hot chocolate and biscuit table.

A perfect night at cubs would be an hour of bulldog followed by half an hour at the tables. The kids'ud go home immaculate. Parents would actually apologise for not sending them tidy in the first place. But that wasn't all. Time they'd done the tables they would've earned a whole sleeveful of badges as well. First-aid, sewing, tea-making, domestic care - you name it, they got the badge. And they didn't take them home for their mums to leave on the side and forget about. No way. They stitched them on at the sewing table the night they got them. A few months with Jewel, they'd be *dripping* with badges, there wouldn't be an inch of sleeve left to sew any more.

Funny thing though. She looked after the cubs, but didn't seem to look after herself. She started to get fat - very fat - and didn't care a bit. It was as if she was proud of her huge belly. She was proud.

Jewel was pregnant.

Didn't leave straight away though. First she got the cubs their nappy-folding badge, baby-bathing badge and teething badge. Then she left.

For a couple of weeks the pack was stuck without a leader. They'd turn up, but there'd be no-one to take them. Then a replacement Akela was found, and when they got there next time the lights were on and in they ran.

A man was standing there. Black hair over his forehead, neckerchief back to front so the triangle looked like a bib, and a parrot on his shoulder. Actually it wasn't a parrot, it was a cockatoo with a twirling crest on its head and a bright yellow beak. When they came in it spread its wings, made a loud squawk, and brought them to a standstill.

'Dib de dib, dob de dob,' the man said, 'I'm your new Akela.'

'Wark!' said the cockatoo. 'Arkey malarkey, arkey malarkey...'

'You can shut your beak,' he said flicking it. 'Douglas, that's me. Douglas the dogless, or Douglas the legless - dog wrapped its lead round my leg and dragged us both in the road. Bus. Went straight over. That's why I've got this thing.' He poked the cockatoo in the breast, making it flutter. 'Damn sight safer than dogs, take my word... Don't believe me, do you? Here...'

Before they could decide if they believed him or not, he rolled part of his baggy trousers up and there was a completely artificial leg.

The cubs were rooted. Hmm. He was different alright.

'Right,' he said, holding up a carton, 'thirty tea bags hidden round the hut. Back in the box. Five minutes...' He waved it as he spoke. The lid flapped.

'Wark!'

It spread its wings and pecked it. No-one moved.

'GO.'

They shot for the corners of the hut like they'd been poked with a cow prod.

'He's bloody barmy,' said Roderick Sodstacker lifting a bench. There was one underneath.

It was a good game though. Last one was in the piano. They nearly took it apart to get it.

They were filthy.

'Right,' said Douglas. 'Two bowls warm water, one soapy one clear, at the double!'

The cubs knew about this with Jewel. They got the table out and fetched the bowls. They rigged the clothesline up and got the pegs. They plugged the iron in.

'Ironing tea-bags?' said Douglas. 'Daft that is. You only rinse 'em - get the dust and cobwebs off. And here we go...' He took a tea-bag by the corner, held it up and began.

'Ha dipdy-do, it goes in here and it comes out here, it goes in there and it comes out there, up to your nose.. smells like a rose.'

He pegged the dripping tea-bag to dry.

'Right, make a line. First one forward. GO... Ha dipdy-do, it goes in here and it comes out here...'

With a shrug the boys joined in, dipping the tea-bags and pegging them to dry. The cockatoo was in paradise. The little bags with their pegs looked like a whole flock of baby cockatoos, and it hopped back and forwards fussing over them.

'Excellent work, excellent work,' said Douglas. 'Soon be ready for drinking. Right. Relay races. Two teams. At the double.'

Stewart hung back. He didn't fancy relays. Luckily the teams were even without him.

'Mr Douglas,' he said, 'um, Akela... could I do a badge?'

'Oh,' he said. 'Badges, is it?' He took him to the door. 'See that tree? Don't take your eye off it, not for a second.'

And off he went.

The relays finished, and the rest of them began to pack up. Stewart stayed at the door, like he'd been told. Douglas made himself a cup of tea and came over, slurping.

'Decent tasting tea, this. Clean as a pin. Well, is it still there?'

'Pardon?' said Stewart.

'The tree. Still there, then. Hasn't moved?'

Stewart hadn't moved, never mind the tree. He was stiff as a board.

'No. It's still where you said.'

'Very good,' he said. 'VERY good. Observers badge for you.'

J210,861.

Stewart looked at him, closely, like he'd done the tree. And he knew Roderick was right.

He was as mad as a mongoose.

Chapter 31
ACCRINGTON STANLEY
WIN THE CUP

Stewart couldn't wait for the next cub night. Nor could the other kids in town. Dozens of them. Douglas the dogless had got more new recruits in one night than the last ten years. The hut was packed.

The cockatoo scarpered off his perch when they charged in. He flew to the rafters and stayed there.

Douglas wasn't bothered – didn't seem to notice the numbers had trebled. He stood in the middle and waited till they were in.

'Right. Make a ring, chop chop,' he said. 'Dibdy-dib, dobdy-dob...'

'Wark!' The cockatoo unloaded a chalky white plop from his new perch. It went quiet for the first time. The dropping was something to look at.

'Snail races,' said Douglas. Producing a stick of chalk he made one side of the ring of kids *elongate*. The movement startled the cockatoo. It sent another dropping down.

'Perfect,' said Douglas. He joined the cockatoo plops with a chalk line.

He crossed to the other side, making them move back, and drew a second line.

'Start - Finish,' he said, straightening up. 'Snail search parties, line up. One two one two one two. At the double.'

'One two one two,' came a voice from the rafters. He was getting his confidence back.

'And you can shut your beak,' said Douglas. The cockatoo shuffled away. A line of twos stretched from the door.

'Be your partner,' said Stewart, grabbing Roderick. There was no way he was going to be odd one out, not after the tree observing.

'And... wait for it... Snail search, five minutes maximum, com...MENCE.'

A hundred shoulders thumped the door frame and shoved out.

The bit outside was overgrown now. There was a broken shed where tools had been kept. If you lifted anything - planks, bricks, bits of roofing - there were tons of snails. Wonder if they're cousins Stewart thought. He had a flower pot full and was sharing them like popcorn. Soon everyone had some. Trouble was, when you put them down and tried to pick your *top sprinters*, they all looked the same. It was hard to tell them apart.

The hut wasn't just used for cubs and scouts. They had mums' keep fit and playgroups. There were paint squeegies in the cupboards. Gary Opengate did blue and white on his. 'Look,' he said. 'Sheffield Wednesday.' It bubbled in his hand.

'Cor!' said Stewart. 'Where?'

'By the sink. Anyone knows.'

He ran over with Roderick. They did Watford and Wigan. Soon everyone was doing them. They had half the teams in the league, plus some extras. They tipped them in the wash-up bowl for a cup draw. 'Number one – Rushden & Diamonds – number two – West Bromwich Albion. Number three – Shrewsbury Town – number four – A.C. Milan...'

Each race was a knock-out between two teams. Snails. Whoever lost went out the door, whoever won went back in for the next round. There were no replays. If they hadn't moved after half a minute - toss of a coin. The cockatoo watched. There were brilliant coloured snails everywhere, it was like the jungle. He flew from his perch and strutted about, pecking one occasionally to see if it was ripe.

There were Cup upsets all night. Palace had a two-inch lead, when the ring collapsed. They copped it under someone's knee - crushed in the first round.

The Premier teams were doing badly. Man United climbed on Burnley's back and got disqualified. Chelsea hid up a table-leg. Arsenal turned out to be dead but reached the semis on the toss of the coin.

It came to the Final. Stoke City v. Accrington Stanley. The *Potters* were in front. Their class was showing. The cubs screamed at the tops of their voices. Accrington stuck his horns out and did a millimetre of slime. Wasn't enough. Douglas had the whistle at his lips, ready to blow.

Oh, you can eat them, thought the cockatoo, thinking it was a snail. He gave Accrington a massive peck, bowling him through the finish as the final whistle went. There was pandemonium. Accrington Stanley – last second of stoppage-time. The Cup heads for *Livingstone Road* for the first time since football began.

'Right,' said Douglas, first one-legged ref since football began, 'chop chop chop, chuck em out, at the double, natural habitat and all that tommyrot.' In a jif the finest teams of England and Europe were scooped up and tossed outside. 'Cept poor old Palace, who were wiped with a cloth and flushed down the loo.

By now the cockatoo had figured snails weren't food, but the bright colours had brought his wildness back. He followed outside and scratched the dirt like mad. Soon he'd found a rusty bike clip, jamjar and a couple of potatoes.

Douglas stood at the door.

'There's gold in this ground,' he drawled. 'Digging parties at the double, dibdy-dib...' Before they knew it they were back out scraping round tree roots for buried treasure.

The old shed had rusty tools. They turned the soil over and over.

'No gold here, Akela,' said Stewart at last, 'just potatoes.' They were tiny - not much bigger than peanuts half of them - but they still filled the bucket.

'Ah-hah!' His eyes gleamed. 'That's your gold. Dirt and tatties - keeps the world alive. Camp-fire party, chop chop. Wood collection – com.. MENCE.'

They didn't have to chop it, it was rotten anyway. Soon they had a decent fire. The spuds were bubbling a treat.

They sat with hands full of hot spuds, fresh from the pan. It was quality nosh. The cockatoo went from cub to cub, stuffing itself. It had found something to eat at last.

'Wark!' it said to Roderick, calling for one.

'Wark!' said Roderick.

'You can shut your beak,' said Stewart. He threw one at it. It hit the next boy. He chucked some back. Next thing there was the mother and father of a spud fight.

The cockatoo squawked like barmy, he'd never seen such a swarm. A big one donged against the bucket. It tilted, and slowly tipped its water on the fire.

There was a great steaming shoosh, and silence. The cubs realised the stars were out. It was dark.

They tumbled back in to get ready, and there sat a lady. Holding something, precious.

Jewel. She'd brought her baby for them.

They crowded round. No-one touched.

'Wark!' squawked the cockatoo, softer. It was back on Douglas's shoulder. As if in time a tiny hand came out, and found Stewart's sleeve. He kept still, the little fingers clutching tight, like a baby bird clutches a branch the first time.

'What's his name?' whispered someone, not to scare him.

'Haven't decided,' said Jewel. Her voice was sweet, like honey.

'Stanley,' someone said. They laughed. Can't give your kid a snail's name, even if it did win the Cup.

'I know...' It came before Stewart could stop it. Then they were waiting.

He blushed.

'Gemma,' he said.

The name floated down and came to rest. Yes. She was a girl. Jewel and Gemma. The little fist released its grip and grew a thumb. She had a tiny mouth, like a kitten's. The thumb went in.

Gemma. Named on Snail Cup Final Day.

Chapter 32
PORTLY PAUL
SAVES THE DAY

Hurricane *Gilbert* was on the tele. Newsflashes interrupted programmes. The main news had cars being blown over gardens and roofs coming off. It made chaos in the West Indies, then gathered speed and smashed into Florida.

Disneyworld was blown to bits. Rides that cost millions strewn like toys after a fight in the garden. Even Cinderella's Castle was gone - dashed to the ground.

People abandoned their homes and fought for places in the *safe havens* inland, where tents and camp beds were layed out for them.

Trouble was, it just kept blasting further and further till it came to the tents, which it blew across the next state, leaving thousands of families in their pyjamas.

We don't get hurricanes here, but the sight of tents whirling in the sky like great fruit bats wasn't too reassuring when Douglas the Dogless announced Cub Camp would be the following weekend. The parents had the feeling you didn't need hurricanes when he was around. He could cause a fair bit of *turbulence* himself.

So they had a meeting and chose an assistant Akela to go with him, in case.

The chap they chose was big. It would take more than a strong wind to blow *him* over. He was massive. He stood by Douglas as they arrived with their torches and bags. You couldn't see his face clearly, he had one of those brown scout hats with the brim shading his eyes. Only thing you could see properly was a pair of huge pink knees poking from his shorts like pumpkins.

I know those knees, thought Stewart. Only one person could have knees that size.

Portly Paul.

He'd stuffed the mini-bus full. It was rammed with food - great catering packs - anything you could think of. The cubs had to strap their gear on the roof, it was the only place. The bus set off like a cross-channel ferry, didn't reach thirty miles an hour till it came to a downhill bit. Trouble was - time they reached the bottom they were screaming along like a race-car. Then they took the hill the other side and almost ground to a halt. It was like a roller coaster. When they got there the cubs were as grey as Douglas's cockatoo, and ready to be sick.

Didn't stop them telling jokes till one in the morning though.

They pitched a *marquee* tent big enough to take breakfast tables and store all the food. It was huge. The pegs holding it down were like cricket bats. It was the Hilton Hotel of tents.

Round it were grouped the cubs' sleeping tents, like moons dotted round the mother planet. The Akelas were in the mini-bus. Portly Paul had unbolted some seats and stacked them in the field to give himself room. Douglas was curled in the driver's place. The cockatoo perched proudly on top, the curl of his crest lit by the moon, like a lord. The last giggles and snores died, and the tired treckers fell in a deep peaceful sleep.

Except Stewart. With all the excitement, his dreams were what you might call active - they were going haywire. New ones would start before the old ones finished. One minute there'd be a cockatoo on his finger, then a little pink hand. There was a subuteo game, but the players turned to painted snails; the ball was a potato, they climbed over, covering it with slime, they climbed over each other; their shiny trails went up and down like a roller coaster, it *was* a roller coaster, a huge one, miles off ground pounded by the wind; cubs whooshed down and up the other side, spires went giddily by - Cinderella's Castle, Disneyworld - the wind howled and shook, bits of frame broke off and swirled away, they were spinning in space...

'Wark!'

Hurricane Gilbert.

Stewart sat up in panic. The wind was beating the tent-sides making them flap like a galleon sail. It had blown across the Atlantic in the night and reached our shores.

There was a shattering crash. A table was over in the marquee, strewing the ground with plates, cans, pots and pans. The cubs came out, torches flickering as if the light beams were being buffeted too. The marquee's canvas rolled and roared like a man o'war, its poles creaked and swayed, lamps clanged from their hooks.

Once the cubs were out, not even their small weight was keeping their own tents down. With a huff the first was airborne, shooting for the trees down the field like a sky-dragon, leaving a few shreds of groundsheet and some pegs.

Another went, another, two more. They swooped and swirled like crows in a gale. Each time one disappeared, it gave the wind more space to drive in and attack the rest.

The marquee was a ship on the rocks. Tins of biscuits, toilet rolls, all the provisions were careering down the field, trying to prong themselves on the barbed wire at the end - and that didn't look like it would last long either.

'Pole-holding parties, at the double, chop chop chop...'

Douglas's pyjamas had ladders and firemen on. His shouts were whipped by the wind and whirled away. No-one heard, they just had to follow, heads down, forcing a path to the marquee. He got them round the poles, holding on. The wind raged and roared and the poles rocked, but it

was the only place standing. They had to keep it secure. Were they holding the poles down, or were the poles holding them down? No-one was sure. They hung on anyway. Boxes of tuck were still taking off, half bouncing, half flying, out the door-flap and away.

Portly Paul wasn't the fastest man on legs, but no way was he giving up his carefully chosen grub without a fight. He charged round rescuing boxes, dragging them through the wall of wind to the van. The seats he'd unbolted had vanished - where was anyone's guess, wedged in forks of trees probably, nice and comfy for the woodpeckers.

All night Portly Paul chased boxes and brought them back. If the cubs could have helped they would have, but he was the only one to be sure not to get carried off by the gale. An earthquake wouldn't have got him off the ground, never mind the wind. Nor a volcano. If he sat on one that was about to *blow-off*, it'ud probably give up and go back to sleep.

When he'd fetched all the eats he could find he went after the tents. He heaved himself up trees, busting branches, and dragged them down one by one. The wind wrenched and tugged, but Portly Paul hung on. He looked like the demon of the storm with sheets and guy-ropes billowing behind him, and the cubs wet themselves with fright. But they clung to the poles.

Finally, the first glimmers of dawn prised the black apart, and the wind dropped. It was safe. The cubs slid to the ground exhausted. The rescued bedding was dragged from the van and flung down. It was a heck of a mess, ripped and tattered, but they grabbed what they could, wrapped it round, and fell without words into bottomless sleep.

Hundreds of years later they woke. The marquee was lit by blazing mid-day sun, and smells of food and charred wood wafted round them. The ragged mounds stirred and became cubs again, and emerged into the brilliant day. Pots of grub bubbled.

'Wark!' squalked the cockatoo. He'd made it, but only just. He was minus some tail feathers, and had a job keeping balance, but at least he was there. Which was more than you could say for Portly Paul. He was nowhere to be seen. Douglas the Dogless had another chap with him, a slim, athletic bloke, turning sausages and serving food. They hadn't seen him before.

Poor old Portly Paul. Must have collapsed with exhaustion, or maybe a huge branch had crashed on top of him. To think, all they'd done was hang on to poles and zonked as soon as the wind dropped, leaving him to work through the night alone. Maybe he was on an operating table that very minute being pieced back together, and all they could do was think about their bellies. Guiltily they held up plates and let the new chap stack them with food.

Stewart came away from the line. He looked at his plate and frowned. It was crammed to the edges, even his thumb was covered in beans.

Hang on, he thought, only one bloke does portions like that... He turned and stared. It was him. Portly Paul. He'd done that much charging after sleeping bags and stuff the pounds had dropped away, and there he stood – slim and fit as an Olympic champion.

Chapter 33
BATTY GOES SHOPPING

Like I said, Stewart wheedled four birthdays in a year, so he figured to lie low and not mention the word again for a while. But that was before Hurricane Gilbert put the wind up him. And I don't mean when it whisked his tent to the tree-tops, either. I mean it got him thinking - what if the storm had whisked *him* up as well, and hung him over a couple of *high-voltage* wires from a pylon? He'd have had his chips.

He reckoned it would be best to get the next birthday in, and on the first decent day, when the sun was shining and the daffs were out, he announced it.

On the *preordained* morning he came down to find a big parcel waiting. There were holes in the top and scratching noises.

'Mouse in my chocolate box - SHOO!' he said. He rushed over and bashed the side. The scratching stopped. Portly Paul and Bertha always got him a chocolate box, and watched hungrily as he opened it.

But the mouse was still there - he could hear it - or something small and nibbly, probably stuffing its cheeks right now. Stewart ripped the paper off. Sure enough, through the holes he could see its eyes and whiskers.

'Right you...' He yanked the top off. 'Oh...' He reached his hands in, and gently lifted it out.

A kitten.

It miowed a little miow, settled in the crook of his arm, and fell asleep purring like a watch. It was his.

As you know, kittens don't lie about for long. They wake up, have a sniff round then start to get frisky. First time Stewart held his hand out, the kitten sniffed it and let itself be picked up. Same the second time. But the third time, it was off, round the settee and up the curtains. Right up. It got to the top like a shot and clung there, face turning one way then the other like an owl, not sure how to get down.

'Catty. You'll get me in trouble...' Stewart whispered. But it dug its claws in as deep as it could and hung on, staring with wild blue eyes.

His first steps in the world of cat ownership hadn't been too successful.

'You ought to call him *Batty*, never mind Catty,' Portly Paul said at breakfast, when they'd got him down. He was mad alright. The curtains were his best place. Every night they'd leave him tucked in his basket by the radiator, every morning he'd be up the curtains again, hanging like a little bat, ears twitching to pick up every sound.

Patsy went potty. There were tiny forget-me-nots on the curtains, she'd sewn them herself. They weren't for cats to hang from.

'What if it gets bigger,' she said. There was no way it could get smaller, it was only the size of an egg to start with. 'It'll bring the whole *pelmet* down.'

She had a point. Cats are strong when they grow. They had to think of something.

They got a collar, and looped it round the chair-leg. Next day he was up there like before. He'd chewed through it. They gave him food before bedtime, so he'd be too full for climbing. First couple of nights it worked, he was that full he couldn't make the sofa never mind the curtains. But he managed the third night. Trouble was, he had such a bellyful of food - time they found him he'd slid back down and there were long rips from his claws. It was no good, he had to be moved.

They tried the pantry, at the back of the kitchen. Wasn't exactly the Ritz, but at least it was warm, and it had one advantage. No curtains.

Next day he was on top of the door. The door was plain wood. Even a cat paw could push it open. It became his kind of tree. First thing they'd see in the morning would be his little white socks over the top, then his ears, then his face, scrutinizing them as they came in.

Batty was not an ordinary cat. He followed Stewart everywhere. Even followed him to Asda when Patsy sent him for some things for the weekend.

Some cats are like that. They've been taken from their mums too soon, so they adopt another mum. And they stay right close to make sure they don't get taken from that one as well. And Batty adopted Stewart. Funny looking mum, but Batty didn't mind so long as the cuddles kept coming.

So when he went to the shops, Batty was there. Stewart shooed him back, but he hid round wheeley bins and under cars. Only thing to do was pick him up and tuck him down his coat. He could feel the purrs.

Didn't suit Batty for long though. He popped his head out as they were crossing at the lights. Well, should have been, but they weren't working. A traffic policeman was directing things, wearing white gloves. He waved them over. Batty poked out a paw and took a couple of baps at his fingers, but he was too busy sorting cars to take a statement.

Stewart popped him in the trolley to go round. When he looked out there was another cat staring, from its master's trolley. They were in the fruit and veg part which had mirrors, and he'd seen himself. But Batty didn't know about mirrors.

Wow – cats' playground, he thought, and jumped out to greet his new friend. The pile of oranges he landed on gave way. His friend's pile gave way too. They rolled on the floor making shoppers swerve and shout. His friend leapt off with a screech. Batty did the same.

He was in a carrot tray now. His friend had stopped to look at something shiny, hanging down. Batty looked too. They jumped and got it with their paw. It uncoiled and slithered down. Snake! They leapt to the floor and skid-daddled, leaving a pile of plastic bags unravelling from its roll.

By now Batty had lost his friend *and* Stewart. He was stuck in a herd of humans by the looks of things, in danger of being trod on.

There were some round shiny steps. He ran up fast as he could. Instead of going somewhere else they stopped. He was on top of a baked-bean tin stack, about to fall. He took a blind leap. The tins collapsed under trolleys and people's feet. He landed on the spaghetti packs. When they crinkled he ran higher. When there was no higher the packs slid under him and fell in the isle as well.

Batty was off. Nowhere was safe in this place, it was like the jungle. He wanted his mum, his Stewart-mum. But his Stewart-mum had seen the bedlam Batty was causing and decided to head for the exit. He wasn't exactly *abandoning* Batty, just getting the heck out before the manager came. He dashed through and aimed for the doors.

Batty made it to the check-out. He jumped up, thinking it was a table. Through the huge window he saw something he recognised. The white gloves of the policeman directing traffic. The till snapped open, the band moved him along with the next person's shopping.

This is no place for a cat, thought Batty. He sprang down and ran at the window. Must be an opening somewhere. The till-girl punched her bell for the manager. There was a pile of boxes. Batty jumped up. They tumbled down.

'OY!'

A man in a suit came after him. The double doors opened for a customer. Batty felt the air and ran.

He was in the street. Wasn't much better, but it was away from the shop-place. There were still feet though, and strange creatures in the road that made hoots when they got angry. He caught sight of the traffic-cop's gloves moving and flicking like a couple of doves and decided they'd be something to attack.

He bolted up his leg, along his arm, and dug his teeth as deep as he could into the gloved hand. He was determined to get something and give it a damn good chomp for all his bother.

'YEOW!' The policeman jerked in pain. Batty bit harder. He tried to swat him with the other hand. Batty bit that as well. The lines of cars couldn't figure if it was their turn or not. Not wanting to get *fined* they nosed forward till there was no road left, just a snarl-up of papping motors, and a policeman doing a jig slap in the middle, completely off his trolley.

Stewart could see this, from way down the road. His conscience was giving him grief. You can't abandon him, it said, he trusts you. I know, Stewart said back, but I think if I get the shopping home first, and maybe have some cornflakes, *then* come and get him, see? That would be best. No, said his conscience, how can you leave him? He thinks you're his mum. He needs you. You know what? I think you're a bit of a *coward*.

Stewart looked back. It was right - he *was* a coward... Who was right? There was no-one else there. He stared, longing to go back, but scared of the dancing copper.

You may not know this, but cats have a sixth sense. They seem to be aware when there's danger, and they know how to get out of it. And Batty was in big danger. The traffic-cop was foaming at the mouth. Batty looked from the wildly waving arm he'd hooked himself to, and way past the shoppers and tooting motorists, spotted two familiar eyes.

Stewart.

In a flash he was over the car tops and gone. Next minute his little face popped out of a privet hedge and looked up.

45

'Batty!' whispered Stewart, though they were miles from the mess they'd caused. 'Quick, in the bag.'

Like I say, cats have a sixth sense. They don't waste much time either. One leap and he was in with the shopping. He might have got bumped by his human-mum's knee a few times as *s/he* legged it for home, but he was safe and in the clear at last.

Chapter 34
STEWART AND
THE FOREST CREATURE

Portly Paul, Bertha, Patsy, Stringy Simon and Stewart were big ones for holidays. They'd been to America and met the President, they'd stayed with the Murdochs in Sydney, they'd ridden the Anglesey Steam Traction Company rolling stock; they'd helped crack the London gemstone robbery and they'd been a couple of rounds with Hurricane Gilbert. Whenever the chance came for a few days away, they'd be up for it. So when Easter came round, and things went quiet at the toy hospital, it seemed the perfect chance to *slip off* for a peaceful weekend youth hostelling in Scotland.

*   *   *   *   *

'Right,' said Portly Paul lobbing his haversack on the top window bunk when they got there, and breathing deeply. 'This is the life.' There was a spare bunk beneath for someone. No way, thought Stewart, heading for a different one by the door. He emptied his things and claimed it.

They laid out their pyjamas, toothbrushes and torches and looked at each other. The bunk-frames were medium blue, the walls were light blue, the window frames were dark blue. Whoever'd painted it knew a thing or two about colour. On the door were the rules, and a picture of the *Matterhorn*, which it's every youth hosteller's dream to climb.

'I'm bored,' said Stewart.

'Bored in Scotland?' said Portly Paul. 'Nonsense. We'll go for a nice walk in the heather after tea, you'll feel like a new man.'

'Haven't got 'nyone to play with...'

'Play with...' said Portly Paul. 'Hmm. Better see if we can find you a friend then... Leave it to me.'

There are places up north where it never gets dark in summer - you can go out at night and see owls and bats and night-time creatures. But this wasn't summer, and though they started in bright evening light, by half-way darkness had fallen like a stone.

Just before it got completely black a creature from the pinewoods trotted up. It nuzzled its head on Stewart's waist.

'Must be a young deer,' said Stringy Simon. The dusk *enveloped* his words and shrunk them to a whisper. 'The famous red deer of Scotland.'

But it wasn't a red deer, it was a little goat. It had appeared from nowhere. Stewart gave his wiry fur a good old scratch. It looked back with its alligator eyes, and gave him a special crackled bleat.

'Ow...' said Stewart in his pleadingest voice. 'Can we...?'

'No,' said Patsy, 'they get fleas. Anyway, he belongs to someone. Now keep up with the rest - it's nearly pitch dark.'

Much as he wanted to stay and cuddle his goaty friend, there was no way Stewart was going to fall behind in *this* place. You get trolls in the forests of the north and a child on his own would be just the ticket for them. They'd encircle him and carry him down to their world.

He caught up sharpish. Portly Paul had his Youth Hostellers' pen-torch out now, and was guiding them back. Least he thought he was. It was getting cold. There was black, and there was very black. Sometimes a night-creature would let out a strange cry.

'Can't be far...' whispered Portly Paul.

Can't it, thought Stewart. There's no such thing as near and far in the kingdom of darkness... As if to prove him right they became aware of a small tapping sound behind, seeming to follow. When they stopped to listen, it stopped. When they started, it started too.

Sounded like... could it be?... a long bearded goblin with a knobbly stick.

'Oh dear. I think...' quivered Stringy Simon in his quietest whisper, quiet like the tiniest breath of breeze through pine needles, 'I think we might have company...'

Not a word passed between them, only the crunch of footsteps, their short scaredy breaths as they huddled together, and the occasional screech of an owl on the hunt for some small creature to tear apart in its talons.

The tap-tapping continued, always behind. The moon came out cold and silver, and went back in the dark. They came to a gate they didn't remember, but not daring to turn back they went through.

'Make sure you shut it,' said Stringy Simon, his voice marbled with dry spit. Stewart gave it a shove and caught up, in case the troll trapped him in the wall-less caverns of dark.

At last, a small light appeared, and they tumbled pell-mell, beating back the soundless night with their footsteps.

'Have you removed your shoes?' said the notice on the door. 'Hostellers must ensure mud remains outside.'

The hell with that, thought Portly Paul, clattering through in his hiking boots. He wanted to be tucked up in his blanket, and the others felt the same. They'd had a bit of a scare.

They clomped upstairs clicking lights on and off, running water and flushing the loo, till at last they were in bed. The knifeblade of forest-dark was outside, and the warm, fuggy people-dark was inside, the way it should be. Gradually their bodies unwound and sleep snuggled in.

About this time Stewart heard tapping again. First he thought it was a hosteller downstairs. He was nearly asleep anyway and didn't care much. But next minute he was wide-eyed and razor-sharp. The tapping sound was at the door. He stopped breathing. His heartbeat kept on. The door opened an inch. There was still breathing, heavy, inhuman. Not his. The hostel dark thinned and froze like the outside dark.

If only he hadn't changed from Portly Paul's bunk he'd be safe now. Well, safe from trolls anyway, if not from twanging springs overhead. But he'd moved by the door, and though the tapping had stopped the snorty breathing was right near. If only he'd slid the bolt across - or before, if he'd shut the gate properly, that might have slowed it down. But he'd been too scared, and now, when he should have been safe, the door slid open a little more and a dark shape entered.

Trolls and goblins are short creatures with dwarfish legs. It occurred to Stewart, even in his terror, that a bunk-ladder would be hard for one to climb.

But it would wait, cause trolls are cunning, till in his sleep Stewart might carelessly let an arm or foot dangle. Then it would pounce.

Scrunching into the middle of the bunk, he clenched his eyes shut and willed himself to sleep. If he could stay tucked-up the troll would have nothing to grab, then when dawn came it would have to give up and join its elfish friends in their world.

Stars glittered in the curtainless window. From the bunk below came a scruffle of bedding. Was it looking for a way up? Stewart scrunched his hands in his ears till a sort of rushing sound filled them, and kept them there. He thought he was going to burst.

*   *   *   *   *

When he let go he was surprised to see daylight. The only breathing was the sleepy kind coming from other bunks. He'd managed to nod off after all, even half-scared out of his wits.

He whipped the bedclothes back and looked down. Under the blanket was a small, breathing shape. The troll! It had waited too long. It was trapped, only a youth hostel blanket to protect it from searing daylight.

Stewart sprang down. He flung the blanket back. There was a flurry. The thing leapt out and faced him with wild yellow eyes.

Goaty. Of course. Following. Whole night in terror of a little goat, now it was in terror of him, doing the only thing a baby goat knows when it's trapped and cornered. It lowered its head. Under the wiry tufts of hair were two little stumps. Its first pair of horns. It was bracing itself to butt him.

'Aah...' Stewart put his hand out and gave them a scratch. It flinched like crazy and did a pile of soft black conkers on the floor. But as he took his hand away it nudged up close and let him scratch and scratch to his heart's content.

Stewart had a friend.

Chapter 35
A TRUE SCOTSMAN

Ever since Portly Paul had been made deputy Akela, he'd started taking *outdoor pursuits* a bit seriously. It was his idea to come to Scotland, and his idea to have the dormitory windows open at night to blow the cobwebs away. Invigorating, he called it - flippin' perishing was Stewart's word, he couldn't get warm no matter how much he snuggled down.

Youth hostels are half-way between a hotel and an army barracks. They've got wooden floors, wooden doors with latches, wooden benches to sit on. They've got bunk-beds with steel frames and blankets made of horse-hair. You sleep ten in a room. You get stream water to wash in, in youth hostels, and tin lids for mirrors. You make your own food but they encourage you to share. That's why the smallest saucepan cooks for twelve.

They don't have tele, they have quiet rooms where you can read about hill-climbing or play dominoes. Don't have chambermaids either. You do chores yourself. There's loads to do at a youth hostel. You can sweep the dormitories, wash up, scrub the kitchen, wipe tables, clean toilets - lots of things to stop you getting bored.

You could tell which bunk was Portly Paul's. The mattress-bit, the base, was beginning to *sag* like a hammock though they'd only been there a night. Tough on anyone who had to have the bottom bunk, it would be like sleeping under a Jumbo-jet, or maybe just a jumbo.

Portly Paul's top bit of kit was his fur-lined walking boots he'd picked up in a sale. He placed them proudly under the bunk before settling down at night. In the morning, while the rest were doing chores, Stewart's job was to clean them with *dubbin* to keep the wet out.

The rules were pinned on the walls in different languages, and though they didn't mention goats by name it was clear pets weren't allowed, and Goaty had to go. The woods weren't so frightening in daytime, and he trotted away as soon as he saw where he was.

Beyond the line of trees a mountain rose serenely to the sky. It looked so inviting in the morning air Portly Paul knew it had to be climbed.

Stewart wasn't bothered about the mountain. All he could think of was his little mate. He sat on his own wondering when he would ever find someone he could really play with.

'We'll find you a friend,' said Portly Paul, clomping in in his fashion walking boots and cagoul. 'A real Scotsman.'

Stewart eyed him thoughtfully.

'How d'you know I'll like him?'

'Course you'll like him,' boomed Portly Paul. 'Best kind of friend you can have. Firm, dependable, solid as a rock, you're bound to like him.'

'Is he the same age as me?' asked Stewart.

'Bit older,' said Portly Paul. 'Come on, get your walking things, we'll take you to meet him right now. His name's Ben.'

'Ben who?'

'Ben Dover. Ben Dover and I'll kick yer bum. No, only teasing. You'll be glad I brought you to see him, come on.'

Wasn't long before they were past the pine-woods and way up the lower slopes. His house must be a bit *out of the way*, thought Stewart, beginning to pant, no wonder he wants to make friends.

The road became a
path, then a trail, then
disappeared completely.
They were climbing the
mountain. Before they
knew it, it became so
steep they stopped talking
altogether. It was all they
could do to manage the
next step.

'Not much further,' gasped Portly Paul from a ledge
he'd heaved himself on to. He spoke to the sky - didn't
dare look down in case it made him giddy.

Before Stewart could reply, a great spongy cloud
drifted across and *enveloped* them. They clung to the
mountain like limpets, not daring to move.

You can't hug a trillion tons of rock for too long
without beginning to feel a bit daft. In the end they
inched their way onwards to the top.

They sat there, too tired and frightened to talk. But
before long the cloud drifted away, and there was the
most breathtaking sight they'd ever seen. Whole of
Scotland like a tablecloth. In every direction were tiny
fields and woods, snail-trails of rivers, pencil-line roads,
and far into the distance, the sea. Their eyes swam in its
beauty.

'Well,' said Portly Paul, breaking into the silence, 'you glad I brought you to meet him then?'

Stewart came to, and looked.   The friend.   He'd forgotten.

'Who? I mean, where?' He spun round.

'Ben,' said Portly Paul, 'right here.   You're sitting on him.   Ben Nevis...'

Have you ever been *had*?   That was how Stewart felt, sitting on top of the highest mountain in Scotland, which he'd been tricked into climbing for no reason at all.

I'll get you for that, he thought, as they got ready to go down.

But he knew, when they were back at last and he was soaking his tired limbs in a deep, steamy bath, it was a day he'd remember the rest of his life.

More Stringy

Simon and Stewart stories in

'The Swiss Army Knife'

About Peter Hayden...

Peter Hayden is the author of the 'Stringy Simon' series, 'The Headmaster's Daughter', 'And Smith Must Score...', and other books.

He grew up in Hove and has four sisters – Susan, Rosie, Vinny and Jill – and has also lived in Norway, the Isle of Man and Australia. He is married with three children (Ben, Mike and Carrie) and their house is right by the Severn Valley Steam Railway station in Bewdley, Worcs. He is old.

He has visited hundreds of schools in the U.K. doing talks, readings and writing workshops. Details are available on 01299 403 201.

Hobbies as a little kid (guess – seven true, three false): football, drawing, library monitor, playing up teachers, collecting cigarette cards, chemistry set, choir, reading sisters' diaries, folding clothes carefully and putting in right drawer, scrumping.

Hobbies now (seven true, three false): football, llama-riding, learning German, balti-cooking, skate-boarding, trying to talk cool, tennis, reading, taking the mick, president of W. Midlands Dai-ichi Bonsai Growers' Assoc.

*(Answers: crazyhorsepress.com)

Team: The Seagulls (Brighton and Hove Albion).

About Clint Banbury...

Clinton Banbury is a widely published illustrator and cartoonist whose work has featured in National Trust, B.B.C., English Heritage, Oxford University Press, Pitkin 'Lookout!' series and other children's publications.

Original illustrations and prints are available from his website: clintonbanbury.com

Other books from Crazy Horse Press...

For 11-18yrs, the next books to read when you finish Stringy Simon....

The Day Trip

'Lost and late, they board the wrong boat home, merge with another school, and end up on the wrong side of the Watford Gap. Ah - but Mike and Lee have declared their love; and what a day they've all had.' *(The Guardian)*

Early teens,   £4.99   ISBN 1 903285 67 4

<u>NEW</u>: Sorting the Apples & Pears

Kim is in her last year of primary school, and needs to sort a few people out before she can step into her teens – parents, cousin, uncle, teacher... and that's just for starters.

Early teens,   £4.99   ISBN 1 871870 26 7

Discount Order Form at back ⟶

And Smith Must Score...

'I recommend it to anyone looking for a good footy read.'
(Nick Hornby)

'A wonderful, charming and witty dose of escapist fiction.'
(Derby Co. F.C. fanzine)

'A football supporter's dream of a book.'
(Middlesbrough F.C. fanzine)

Adult & older teen, £6.99 ISBN 1 871870 08 9

The Headmaster's Daughter

'I really enjoyed reading it. It was like listening in on girls' cloakroom gossip.' *(Berlie Doherty)*

'It's the kind of book that you would be sort of drifting with when you start reading it but when you'd finished you'd read it again because you realise how it fits together and appreciate the detail given at the beginning.'

(Teenage reader - original available)

Older teens, £5.99 ISBN 1 871870 09 7

The Poppy Factory Takeover: Teenage Writing

Creative writing in the classroom - observations and examples from three decades of writing with children. Includes two humorous verse stories written by teenagers and illustrated by Clinton Banbury.

'There is about the whole book a trustworthiness which carries it all... I hope it gets reviewed at length in the right places.'
(David Hart, Birmingham Poet Laureate)

Adult & older teen, £6.99 ISBN 1 871870 12 7

Discount Order Form

Pay £4.99 for the first book, and you get all the rest (any title!) for £3.99 each. But there's a better deal over the page. It's your choice...

Complete and send to -

Crazy Horse Press, 53 Stourport Road Bewdley DY12 1BH

Tick Box

☐ One copy of Portly Paul Buys a Bed	=	£_____
☐ One copy of Patsy's Parlour	=	£_____
☐ One copy of Stewart and the Alien	=	£_____
☐ One copy of The Conker Champ	=	£_____
☐ One copy of Stewart and the Forest Creature	=	£_____
☐ One copy of The Swiss Army Knife	=	£_____
☐ One copy of The Day Trip	=	£_____
☐ One copy of Sorting the Apples and Pears	=	£_____
☐ One copy of The Headmaster's Daughter	=	£_____
☐ One copy of And Smith Must Score	=	£_____
☐ One copy of The Poppy Factory Takeover	=	£_____

TOTAL (No postage to pay!) £_____

Galway County Libraries

Name _____

Address_____

_____

Post-Code_____ Phone _____

I enclose a cheque to _Crazy Horse Press_ for £_____

PRINT FIRST NAME HERE_____

– if you would like Peter Hayden to sign your book.

If you order 2 or more copies of books, you must be getting them for your friends - so you get a sales discount for doing the work. All books £3.50

Sales Discount Order Form

[Schools and libraries can use it too - we'll let ya..]

Complete and send to Crazy Horse Press 53 Stourport Road, Bewdley DY12 1BH

Write number here - ones not allowed on this form.
↓

_____	Copies of Portly Paul Buys a Bed	= £_____
_____	Copies of Patsy's Parlour	= £_____
_____	Copies of Stewart and the Alien	= £_____
_____	Copies of The Conker Champ	= £_____
_____	Copies of Stewart and the Forest Creature	= £_____
_____	Copies of The Swiss Army Knife	= £_____
_____	Copies of The Day Trip	= £_____
_____	Copies of Sorting the Apples and Pears	= £_____
_____	Copies of The Headmaster's Daughter	= £_____
_____	Copies of And Smith Must Score	= £_____
_____	Copies of The Poppy Factory Takeover	= £_____

TOTAL (No postage to pay!) £_____

Name _____

Address _____

_____

Post-Code _____ Phone _____

I enclose a cheque to CrazyHorse Press for £_____

✱ If you would like Peter Hayden to sign the books, PRINT EACH PERSON'S FIRST NAME and the books they are having on a separate sheet. He's not too good at reading so make sure your writing is clear!

[Eire, U.S.A., Canada, S.A., Australia, N.Z. - refer to web-site]

xiv

Discount Order Form

Pay £4.99 for the first book, and you get all the rest (any title!) for £3.99 each. But there's a better deal over the page. It's your choice...

Complete and send to -

Crazy Horse Press, 53 Stourport Road Bewdley DY12 1BH

Tick Box

- ☐ One copy of Portly Paul Buys a Bed   = £_____
- ☐ One copy of Patsy's Parlour   = £_____
- ☐ One copy of Stewart and the Alien   = £_____
- ☐ One copy of The Conker Champ   = £_____
- ☐ One copy of Stewart and the Forest Creature   = £_____
- ☐ One copy of The Swiss Army Knife   = £_____
- ☐ One copy of The Day Trip   = £_____
- ☐ One copy of Sorting the Apples and Pears   = £_____
- ☐ One copy of The Headmaster's Daughter   = £_____
- ☐ One copy of And Smith Must Score   = £_____
- ☐ One copy of The Poppy Factory Takeover   = £_____

TOTAL (No postage to pay!) £_____

Name _____

Address _____

Post-Code _____ Phone _____

I enclose a cheque to <u>Crazy Horse Press</u> for £_____

PRINT FIRST NAME HERE _____

   - if you would like Peter Hayden to sign your book.

Sales Discount Order Form

[Schools and libraries can use it too - we'll let ya..]

Complete and send to Crazy Horse Press
53 Stourport Road, Bewdley DY12 1BH

Write number here - ones not allowed on this form.

_____ Copies of Portly Paul Buys a Bed = £_____
_____ Copies of Patsy's Parlour = £_____
_____ Copies of Stewart and the Alien = £_____
_____ Copies of The Conker Champ = £_____
_____ Copies of Stewart and the Forest Creature = £_____
_____ Copies of The Swiss Army Knife = £_____
_____ Copies of The Day Trip = £_____
_____ Copies of Sorting the Apples and Pears = £_____
_____ Copies of The Headmaster's Daughter = £_____
_____ Copies of And Smith Must Score = £_____
_____ Copies of The Poppy Factory Takeover = £_____

TOTAL (No postage to pay!) £_____

Name _____

Address _____

_____

Post-Code _____ Phone _____

I enclose a cheque to CrazyHorse Press for £_____

* If you would like Peter Hayden to sign the books, PRINT EACH PERSON'S FIRST NAME and the books they are having on a separate sheet. He's not too good at reading so make sure your writing is clear!

[Eire, U.S.A., Canada, S.A., Australia, N.Z. - refer to web-site]

Discount Order Form

"Pay £4·99 for the first book, and you get all the rest (any title!) for £3·99 each. But there's a better deal over the page. It's your choice...

Complete and send to -

Crazy Horse Press, 53 Stourport Road Bewdley DY12 1BH

Tick Box

☐ One copy of Portly Paul Buys a Bed = £_____

☐ One copy of Patsy's Parlour = £_____

☐ One copy of Stewart and the Alien = £_____

☐ One copy of The Conker Champ = £_____

☐ One copy of Stewart and the Forest Creature = £_____

☐ One copy of The Swiss Army Knife = £_____

☐ One copy of The Day Trip = £_____

☐ One copy of Sorting the Apples and Pears = £_____

☐ One copy of The Headmaster's Daughter = £_____

☐ One copy of And Smith Must Score = £_____

☐ One copy of The Poppy Factory Takeover = £_____

TOTAL (No postage to pay!) £_____

Name _____

Address _____

_____

Post-Code _____ Phone _____

I enclose a cheque to Crazy Horse Press for £_____

PRINT FIRST NAME HERE _____

– if you would like Peter Hayden to sign your book.

If you order 2 or more copies of books, you must be getting them for your friends - so you get a sales discount for doing the work. All books £3·50

Sales Discount Order Form

[Schools and libraries can use it too - we'll let ya..]

Complete and send to Crazy Horse Press
53 Stourport Road, Bewdley DY12 1BH

Write number here - ones not allowed on this form.
↓

[Eire, U.S.A., Canada, S.A., Australia, N.Z. - refer to web-site]

_____ Copies of Portly Paul Buys a Bed = £_____

_____ Copies of Patsy's Parlour = £_____

_____ Copies of Stewart and the Alien = £_____

_____ Copies of The Conker Champ = £_____

_____ Copies of Stewart and the Forest Creature = £_____

_____ Copies of The Swiss Army Knife = £_____

_____ Copies of The Day Trip = £_____

_____ Copies of Sorting the Apples and Pears = £_____

_____ Copies of The Headmaster's Daughter = £_____

_____ Copies of And Smith Must Score = £_____

_____ Copies of The Poppy Factory Takeover = £_____

TOTAL (No postage to pay!) £_____

Name _____

Address _____

_____

Post-Code _____ Phone _____

I enclose a cheque to Crazy Horse Press for £_____

✱ If you would like Peter Hayden to sign the books, PRINT EACH PERSON'S FIRST NAME and the books they are having on a separate sheet. He's not too good at reading so make sure your writing is clear!